PLOWSHARES

— A —

Contemporary
Fable
of Peace and War

SONIA RALSTON

PAULIST PRESS/NEW YORK/MAHWAH

Library of Congress Cataloging-in-Publication Data

Ralston, Sonia, 1921–
  Plowshares: a contemporary fable of peace and war.

  Bibliography: pp.
  I. Title.
PS3568.A436P54   1986   813'.54   86-2443

ISBN: 0-8091-2788-1

Published by Paulist Press
997 Macarthur Boulevard
Mahwah, New Jersey 07430

Printed and bound in the
United States of America

*For my three sons, about
whose world this story
is told*

"We shall require a substantially new manner of thinking if mankind is to survive."

Albert Einstein

"No cord nor cable can so forcibly draw, or hold so fast, as love can do with a twined thread. . . ."

Robert Burton . . . 1576–1640

Once upon a time, in a faraway land which could be yours or mine, there lived a Man with his wife and young son.

Their dwelling place was set sturdily at the foot of a fold in the hills. Behind it rose the Mountains which embraced this generous Valley and its sweet, clear river.

Their lives, like those of their neighbors, moved in harmony with the seasons. It was a pattern of life followed by all the people.

In spring, when the rich soil first crumbled to the touch, the Woman planted potatoes and sweetcorn, flax for spinning and morning glories to joy the heart. The Man ploughed and sowed his portion of the community Fields, just as his father and grandfather had done. Every contour and outcrop of the land was as familiar to him as the gentle features of his wife's face. Often he sang as he worked.

And the Boy, prompted by a certain new softness in the wind, would lead their small flock of sheep from the winter croft, up into the freshly greening pastures of the lower hillside.

There were honeybees at the homestead . . . a donkey, two milchcows, a rabble of hens, and almost always a kindle of kittens in the byre.

During the long summer days which followed, the Woman labored in the garden, her fingers stained with the juice of tiny mountain strawberries, her flaxen braids damply tendrilled by the midday sun. Each noon she carried bread, some cheese and a gourd of fresh milk to where her husband worked in the Fields with the other men, hoeing and cosseting their burgeoning grain. Sometimes she would tarry with him momentarily, and they would laugh together.

In summer, too, the Boy and his dog moved the sheep and young lambs high up into the Mountain, bringing them to new pasture. Often he was gone for several days, but the Woman did not fret his absence, for as she moved among her hollyhock in the garden below she sometimes caught—over the distant cow-bells and querulous bleating of the lambs—the sweet sound of his wooden pipe on the Mountain above.

Always, as the year
moved forward and
crickets whirred in the

drying wheat, neighbor would join neighbor, companionably working together to bring in the abundant
harvest. Wielding their scythes the men moved in a
mighty line across the Fields, toppling the ranks of
gold with practiced precision. Cut bundles were tied
with twine and placed in shocks to dry. And later in
the threshing house, the women would chatter happily together, a heavy white dust settling on their arms
as they flailed out the glistening kernels. It was the old
men and the boys who winnowed and garnered this
final treasure, piling the heavy sacks in fragrant pyr-
amids within the granary.

When at last it was done, the people of the Valley always gathered in one of the barns to sip wine, dance old reels, and sing the familiar songs.

This was, they agreed yearly, the best of all times. For they were, indeed, brothers and sisters of the soil.

Winters were undeniably hard.

Winds howled up the Valley then, piling snow against the little houses, severing them still further from the Outside World. Animals huddled together in their stalls for warmth, and the bleating of the sheep could be heard at night above the banshee wailing of the shifting roof shingles.

Little work could be done then. Each family rode out the storms alone, praying their stored food and firewood would suffice. During those long evenings the Man always whittled a gift for his wife. Once it was a milking stool inscribed with the words: "My Heart Is Ever With You." And once a fine comb for her flaxen hair.

It was an innocent world.

It could have been a good and perfect life.

But for the one jeopardy which was never wholly out of their minds. . . . . . .

This was
the ever present danger
of the Enemy.

It had always been so.

12

Enemy territory lay on the far, forested side of the Mountain, only a long day's march away, a black mantle of darkling conifers separating the two factions.

Nobody could remember a time when their threatening presence had not colored Valley decisions, intruded upon Valley lives.

Hearsay had it that their language was a threatening babel of low-pitched gutterals, and their appearance was known to be fiercely alien. How long they had been there was uncertain, but the Man could remember his great-grandfather speaking of the hordes which had swept down over the Mountain even when he was a boy, burning and pillaging, carrying off livestock.

The passage of time changed nothing. Even on the sweetest summer evening, when fish were biting and the scent of wild woodbine filled the air, the threat lingered darkly, a hideous cancer constantly feeding beneath the flesh.

And each time the invaders came it was necessary, of course, for the Man and his neighbors to reciprocate in kind.

Always, when he lifted down his gun from its accustomed place above the kitchen mantel—felt the familiar smoothness of the stock, smelled the lingering pungency of old powder—the Man was aware of his father. And his father's father before him. How many times had they, too, achingly reacquainted themselves with that gun's heft? How many times embraced the women and children they loved and moved out to protect them?

"It seems," the Man always thought wearily, "there is no end to it."

The Woman could recall several occasions when she had witnessed him leave thus, joining the other men of the Valley in their farewells.

Each time, for her, it was the same. She would stand at the threshold of their little home, the anguish of his embrace still with her. He'd stride away toward the muster, along the path that led between the daisies and the meadowsweet—his thatch of wheaten hair above the familiar shoulders. Desperately she would try to imprint the feel . . . and smell . . . and taste of him in her memory, fearing she might never experience them again.

Once, as she watched him go, the child she carried moved for the first time within her. She longed to share this quickening of their firstborn with him. But she refrained, knowing his heart to be already breaking.

Repetition never made these departures easier. And, as she knew it inevitably would, the year eventually came when that same firstborn—her beloved eldest son—joined in the going.

Hardly strong enough yet to shoulder the gun his father gave him, the older boy listened as his parents argued:

"Not yet! *Ah! not yet!*"

"It is time. He must go with me. The Elders require it. Sooner or later, like all of us, he will have to learn."

And so the two of them departed, a mismatched pair, along the pathway.

Watching, the Woman saw other men of the Valley come out to join them. Other fathers. Other sons. Together the little band vanished toward the dark conifers of the Mountain ... and the waiting Enemy.

She turned then, and, lifting her second manchild from his cradle, wept until her anguish woke the sleeping infant.

Later, just as she knew he would, the Man returned alone.

Silently replacing the two guns over the mantel, he turned to embrace her and joined his anguished tears with hers.

That night, under cover of darkness, he went once more to the Mountain, and, just when the Woman thought that he also was lost, he returned with the dead boy.

Together they buried his body beside an outcropping of lichened rock beyond the homestead. There was an old apple tree close by, and they knew that in springtime it would gently blanket the grave with fallen blossoms.

In the Aprils which followed, the Woman would gather forget-me-nots along the river's edge and place them beside the grave.

But time healed her heart by not one whit.

Several years passed. As the younger Boy grew—tall and beautiful as a tender oak sapling—there were, between the wars, some happy times again.

Often, in the evening, the father would fish with his son along the river bank in companionable silence. Above them fireflies curtseyed in a courtly pavan, and among the bullrushes sated frogs chorused velvet accompaniments.

The Boy would hurry forward to carry the brimming milk pails for his mother now, just as his older brother once had done, and there was a new, wistful searching in the music of his pipe.

There came a year when springtime seemed even sweeter than ever, the earth particularly rich and dark under the plough, the fruit trees heavy with blossom. Soft rains nourished the new wheat, and the whole Valley appeared alive with green promise.

One day, in that summer which followed, the Boy sat with his flock in a small clearing high up in the Mountain, feeling a great sense of peace.

Lured by a distant patch of gentian and wild narcissus, he had wandered a little farther than usual into the upper reaches. Be-low him the Valley stretched—checkered and orderly in the sunlight. Seen from this new vantage point it felt particularly dear to him.

Turning his back on the alien crags above, he pulled his pipe from his pocket and began to play, in concord with the faint splash of distant waterfall.

Joyful . . . serene . . . the
music lifted among the mountains,
joining the jubilate of a lark.

And then, quite suddenly, another pipe joined his . . .

. . . softly echoing . . .

. . . sweetly poignant . . .

Startled, the Boy took his instrument quickly from his lips and, standing on a rock, scanned the unfamiliar reaches above him.

There, in a distant clearing, surrounded by grazing sheep, pipe in hand, sat a boy like himself.

For a long moment the two surveyed each other across a no-man's-land of rock and gentian—this flaxen youth and his dark echo.

Tentatively the Boy put his pipe to his lips once more and began to play . . .

. . . Across the clear, brittle air the responding notes arose, hesitant at first and then gaining confidence.

Pure . . . . .

innocent . . . . .

holy . . . . .

No words were exchanged that first day. Nor, for some time, did they attempt to approach each other. It was not until one of the lambs became ensnared in a thorn bush that both boys ran to succor it and came face to face at last.

They were never sure from which flock the lamb strayed. It seemed of no importance. Together they held the bleeding, terrified animal in their arms, crooning and comforting in the age-old tongue common to all shepherds.

When at last the little creature fell asleep between them, the boys sat together in the sunlight, playing their flutes. They were profoundly content. Having music, they required no words.

When he returned home that night the Boy did not tell his father of this strange encounter. But the Woman noticed an odd exhilaration about him.

This was the first of many such mountain meetings. Throughout that summer the two flocks grazed companionably together, the sound of pipes in sweet duet about their ears.

Once, in the slow, hesitant gestures of their burgeoning communication, the boys spoke of war:

"Why," gestured one, "do you cross the Mountain to fight us?"

"Because," mimed the other, "we fear you."

"How strange . . . it is even so with us," said the first.

They sat for a long time after that, in puzzled silence.

"But what is there to fear?" asked one at last, shaking his head in bewilderment.

"I do not know," the other answered sadly. "But the Elders say it has always been so. If you become too strong you will attack us."

"But our Elders claim the same," came the soft reply. "If only they would speak together of these things."

That day the two boys parted with heavy hearts.

*   *   *

Summer was drawing to a close. The sun had gilded the wheat's rich green, and the Valley shimmered in the dry heat. Many months had passed since the Enemy's last incursion and the people were filled with hope.

"This should be a splendid harvest," said the Man, standing at the Field's edge with his arm about his wife's waist. "Perhaps there will even be some money left to buy books for the boy."

The Woman smiled. Throughout the past winter she had worked with her son, the two of them hunched over a guttering candle as the wind outside lamented among the chimney pots. Together they marveled at the wonders of the Outside World, exploring tales of chivalry . . . poetry . . . the nature of life itself. This had been a time of great joy for her.

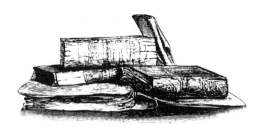

"And a new flute for him also?" she asked her husband now.

"If all goes well," he replied.

"And if," each silently acknowledged, "the Enemy leaves us in peace."

The time came, as it always did, when the Elders, upon consulting customary portents, called for the communal harvesting to begin next day.

"Never," everyone agreed, "has there been such an abundance!"

That night the families of the Valley were early to bed, in happy anticipation of the morrow.

But the expected pleasure was not to be.

During the night the Enemy swept down from the Mountain, burning the fields of wheat, torching haystacks, plundering, savaging.

When, just as abruptly, they withdrew, not one stalk of grain was left standing in the Valley. Only blackened devastation, and the acrid stench of scorched soil. Among the stubble lay the little bodies of frightened hares, trapped by the holocaust.

Not only was the year's harvest lost, but next spring's seed-grain as well. The intruders spared nothing.

Retaliation was swift and total.

By the following nightfall the Enemy's rich fields on the other side of the Mountain also lay in smoking ruins, and an ashy pall blanketed both valleys.

Upon their return, the weary, fire-stinking men were summoned to an urgent council by the Elders. What everyone always dreaded most, they were told, was about to happen. Word had come that the Enemy now planned to invade and take possession of the Valley itself.

"We have no choice," the Elders said. "We must at once sell everything—the sheep, the cows, the bales of wool—and with that money buy from the gunsmiths of the Outside World all the armaments necessary for our protection."

"But how will we then buy seed-grain for next spring?" someone asked.

The Elders conferred briefly together. "What is the use of grain-seed," came their reply, "if we have no land upon which to plant it? Defenseless we are doomed to lose everything to the Enemy."

The people of the Valley sat silent. Some of them had seen it all before. They knew an arsenal enriched meant a schoolhouse impoverished. Once again the sick would be needy, the widows wanting. It was a familiar, desperate choice.

"Perhaps, if we arm mightily," said the Man to his wife that night when he returned home, "word will reach the Enemy of our great new strength and they will be deterred by it".

She shook her head. "It has not stopped them before," she replied quietly.

The Man said nothing. She watched as he lifted down the second, smaller gun from where it had hung ever since that long-ago anguish. Sitting at the kitchen table he began, very carefully, to clean and oil the firing piece. His shoulders drooped and his face was ashen with grief as he worked.

In front of him, on the blue-and-white checkered tablecloth, among the homely crumbs of bread and cheese and beside a jar of faded meadow poppies, he meticulously aligned and divided the two allotments of shells given him by the Elders.

"They are like little regiments of death," the Woman thought to herself.

The Boy stood behind his father's chair, watching silently. "Get some sleep, son," the Man said softly. "We will all be needed on the morrow."

Their guns beside them, the men of the Valley slept deeply that night, exhausted from the day's reciprocal destruction. But the womenfolk stared into darkness, drained by the terror ahead.

Shortly after midnight, the Woman slipped from the warmth of her sleeping husband's side and entered the small room where her son lay.

A shaft of moonlight slanted across his pillow, illuminating the young face, sweaty with sleep . . . the flaxen hair . . . the cheeks tanned by mountain winds.

 About him, all the old, familiar possessions of boyhood . . . a fishing pole . . . a knife . . . some books . . . the shapeless boots and sheepskin vest. Even the odors of the room were uniquely his, causing her heart to break still further.

But it was his pipe, and the gentle fingers still holding it in sleep, which contracted her throat beyond bearing. From closed eyes, tears flowed down her cheeks in the darkness at the thought of so much sweet music soon to be silenced.

When she looked down again at her sleeping son, she noticed for the first time the little fuzz of golden down along his lip.

He was already
almost gone from her.

It was then that the Woman knew, without any doubt, what it was she must do.

Walking quickly back into the kitchen she lifted down the Boy's gun and placed it across the kitchen table. And then, layering the little legions of ammunition punctiliously between folds of a large kerchief, she packed them within her wicker egg basket.

This done, she slipped soundlessly into the room where her husband still slept deeply.

Carefully she lifted his gun from beside the bed.

Irresolute for a second, she stood looking down.

"If I am robbing you of that by which you demonstrate the depth of your love for us, forgive me, my beloved," she begged silently. "Somewhere this madness has to stop."

And then, taking a warm shawl for her shoulders, she left him.

With the two guns cradled in the crook of her arms, the egg basket clasped in her trembling fingers, she stepped out into the moonlight.

Up toward the Fields she went, past the green rock and the apple tree, along the chalky pathway with its night-shuttered poppies and tangled sweetbriar.

Once she paused to look back at the darkened Village, remembering those other women who, within hours, would have to say their own farewells. A great sadness swept over her. "The world is so beautiful," she thought, "and its people so precious. Why is there such anger?"

When at last she came to the Community Fields she was appalled afresh by the devastation which stretched all about her. The blackened earth stank sourly, and a hoot-owl circled overhead, searching for carrion.

Moving to the center of the Fields, she sank to her knees between the charred furrows, and began, as she knew she must, to dismantle the guns.

The task went easily. She had seen it performed a hundred times before, the Man spreadeagling the pieces across the kitchen table, cleaning, oiling, repairing.

As the parts—one by one—came away in her cold fingers, she placed them in a pile beside the egg basket.

Beneath her the stubble pressed against her bare legs, but she worked on, oblivious of all but the mission at hand. Once she thought she heard distant wolves, and looked fearfully at the Mountain looming darkly above her. Again she knew a second's indecision. Would her actions save or destroy those two lives she most treasured?

But she labored on.

The pieces, she knew, must be dispersed beyond recovery, buried where the blades of some future plough would finish her task.

Finally she stood and, filling her broad apron with the severed fragments, moved slowly forward . . .

And so it was that she committed to the soil each nut and bolt, each spring and hammerpin.

With her soft flaxen hair loosed about her shoulders, she moved along the ravished furrows in the moonlight, her motions duplicating the age-old stance of the sower-of-seed.

Polished stocks, burnished barrels, sighting bar and lockpin—the blackened earth received and concealed each sundered part. And finally, one by one, the deadly contents of her egg basket.

It was done.

There was no reversing her actions now.

When her arms were empty at last of their strange burden, she turned at the final furrow and looked back from whence she had come . . .

Motionless in the moonlight she stood,
her eyes wide with disbelief.
And then she began to tremble
greatly at the enormity of what
was unfolding before her . . .

For, stretching in a neat line where she had just passed, pushing between the blackened stubble in a ribbon of newly-disturbed soil, there was emerging a sudden rank of tender green . . .

Incredulous and fearful she watched.

Sturdily the tiny spikelets flourished, swelling and opening even as she gazed.

She reached into her egg basket. Her trembling fingers found metal one more time. Thrusting this final bullet into the soil in front of her, she sank to her knees, clasped her hands over her mouth, and watched in wonderment.

> Like hatching chick, new green
> pressed through the cracking
> soil, thrusting, multiplying,
> reaching up. . . .

When, as she ran homeward, she turned to scan the Fields once more, the line of grain already stood richly full and waist high.

It was not difficult to rouse the other women in the Village. Like her, they had lain wakeful beside their exhausted husbands, dreading the morrow.

They did not question her story. It was as if they had always known it could be so.

They, too, took the guns from their sleeping menfolk, and followed the Woman soundlessly through the moonlight to the Fields.

Kneeling in the stubble they took apart the weapons which had caused them so much anguish, committing the dismembered pieces carefully to the soil. They worked in silence.

Later, returning yet again, they carried from the Village Arsenal the remaining boxes of ammunition on their sturdy backs.

By the time their task was complete dawn was already breaking along the mountains . . . yellow at first, then fading to soft damask.

Once more the great Fields lay about them, heavy in grain. The full ears awaited only the benison of that day's drying sun to bring them to golden fruition.

Upon the return of the women to the Village, the men ran out to meet them:

"We feared the Enemy had come secretly in the night and carried you away!" they cried.

"Where were you? We have been searching everywhere!"

"The Enemy has taken our guns!" shouted another.

When the women told their story the men were, in turn, angry, fearful, and, finally, disbelieving. The Elders, in particular, castigated the women.

"What have you done? *What have you done?* We are defenseless!" they chorused.

But when the whole Village returned to the Fields and saw there the miraculous wheaten ocean shimmering in the morning sunlight, ripening and multiplying constantly even as the incredulous people watched, wonderment overcame anger, and the farmer in each man marveled greatly.

Majestically each sturdy stem grew apace, heavy with kernels.

"In all my years," said one of the Elders, "I have never seen grain like this. It will be the talk of scholars everywhere!"

("Much has gone into the perfecting
of it," thought the Woman to herself,
remembering the green-lichened rock
and the apple blossoms which fell there
in the springtime.)

Fingering the rich, full ears, the Elder went on. "With a seed-strain like this it will be possible to feed the hungry of the whole world!"

"If only," someone in the crowd pointed out, "we could be assured the Enemy will not destroy this too."

"We must harvest it at once," everyone agreed quickly, "before word reaches them on the other side of the Mountain."

And so, throughout that day, the entire Village labored together, men and women, young and old. The dusty air was filled with the rhythmic hiss, hiss of scythe, and the arms of the women moved ceaselessly in the age-old slap-slap of flail against threshing floor.

But even as the menfolk harvested, so new shoots of green thrust through the soil, burgeoning, ripening and drying behind them continuously.

Frantically the villagers toiled, praying the Enemy would not learn of this miracle.

But their fears were groundless.

This time it was the Boy who knew what it was he must do, and he had already left on a journey.

Plucking one splendid stalk of new wheat from the field, he stole secretly back to the homestead and, slipping his pipe inside his vest, set off on the donkey toward the Mountain.

In the familiar sunlit clearing he dismounted, and facing the dark conifers set the pipe to his lips.

His music was answered, just as
he prayed it would be.

Advancing toward each other, the two boys hesi-
tated for only a moment and then embraced. They
stood, holding each other at arm's length, their cheeks
streaked with tears.

"But why, *why?*" each asked of the other.

Lifting the stalk of wheat from the donkey's sad-
dlebag, the Boy gestured his story . . .

"Take it," he said, pressing the sturdy stem into
his friend's hand. "Show it to your mother. Tell her.
She will know what to do."

*   *   *

There is a sisterhood which exists between women.

Perhaps it springs from their certain knowledge that after all the endless words . . . words . . . it is the beloved creation of their own bodies which is cut down by the sniper's bullet. Always a part of them dies too.

And so it was that the womenfolk of the Enemy also stole away to their own fields that midnight, arms heavy-laden with weaponry.

By dawn there was grain—in abundance beyond telling—flourishing and multiplying on both sides of the Mountain. When night fell the storage houses of both peoples overflowed, and the hands of the men and women were blistered by labor.

Still fearful at first, the rivals worked in frenzied secrecy, certain that revelation of the miracle would surely trigger immediate attack. In addition to the wheat they knew would be consumed during winter, each was determined to hide from his enemy enough of the amazing seed-grain to ensure future continuance of the strain next spring. Throughout both villages every earthen crock, trinket-box and hope-chest was pressed into service to conceal this special sleeping gold.

But the days passed peacefully. And soon it was known that each side was familiar with the other's secret.

Clearly there was, after all, enough for everyone.

"The enemy is prospering so mightily, his need for piracy seems quite forgotten!" rejoiced the people on both sides of the Mountain.

*   *   *

Summer drew to a close. Still the self-replenishing harvest overflowed the fields, green following gold following green.

Finally it became obvious to the exhausted laborers of both valleys that in order not to lose any of this prodigious bounty under early snow, it was expedient for these old rivals to unite in their preservation efforts.

Thus, throughout the fading days and nights of that late autumn, a great alliance of ingenuity and brawn sprang up between them to keep pace with the unending profusion.

Working in planned harmony, the men and women moved back and forth between the two valleys, harvesting one day, threshing the next, barely able to keep ahead of the urgently-renewing ranks of green. Oxen and horses were loaned, whetstones shared, storage bins constructed. Together these erstwhile enemies sharpened scythes, mended wheels, compared tools, and often found themselves awed by a sameness in their tongues.

In the homesteads the children and old-folk struggled to keep abreast of the endless demand for new grain sacks, stitching and chattering happily among their new-found friends.

There was laughter in the fields and threshing houses, and even sometimes a shy exchange of song.

Only at the first snowfall did the miraculous greening cease at last.

Their World lay about the People, white and beautiful under its fresh new coverlet.

It was, they agreed, the best of all times. For were they not Brothers and Sisters of the soil?

That is really only the beginning of the story . . .

When, in the April which followed, the Woman walked again along the river bank to gather forget-me-nots, she no longer looked toward the mountain in fear.

Instead she saw how beautiful was the mist over the river . . . the flash of kingfisher among the greening willow-wands . . . the velvet vulnerability of an emerging fern. She smelled the lilacs and the earth's damp pungency, and listened to peepers chattering amid the sedges.

From the mountain high above her, accompanied by the bleat of young lamblings, she heard the sound of her son's new flute.

A second pipe took up the melody, the notes rising in harmony above the sunlit conifers.

The music soared and lifted in the clear mountain air, joyously unafraid.

*   *   *

Credits:

THE ILLUSTRATOR'S HANDBOOK, A & W Visual Library: cover (engraving by Winslow Homer), and pages 6, 17, 46 (both), 47, 52.

NEW ENGLAND BYGONES by E.H. Arr, J.B. Lippincott & Co., 1883: pages 1, 3, 18, 24, 28, 34 top, 55.

ABIDE WITH ME by Henry Francis Lyte, Lee & Shepard, 1878: page 38.

A GUERNSEY LILY by Susan Coolidge, Roberts Bros., 1881: First frontispiece, 2nd frontispiece (haying), 22.

COLONIAL DAYS by Richard Markham, published Dodd, Mead & Co., 1881: pages 12, 16.

SONGS FOR THE LITTLE ONES AT HOME, Mary O. Ward, The American Tract Society, 1852: page 20.

BEGINNER'S FRENCH READER, published Henry Holt & Co., 1868: pages 7, 48.

GRAPHIC ARCHIVES, Ron Yablon, Box 63, Exton, Pa.: cover (bullets only) and pages 1, 15, 34 bottom, 37, 53, 54.

1800 WOODCUTS BY THOMAS BEWICK AND HIS SCHOOL, Dover Publications: page 2.

THE BOYS' BOOK OF SPORTS, published by The Century Co., 1886: pages 19, 36.

JEAN INGELOW'S POEMS, published by Roberts Bros., 1873: facing quotations.

HIGHWAYS & BYWAYS, by William Hamilton Gibson, Harper & Bros., 1883: facing copyright page 5, 59.

HARPER'S NEW MONTHLY MAGAZINE, 1876–1877: page 50.

HARPER'S NEW MONTHLY MAGAZINE, 1877–1878: pages 26, 31.

HILL'S MANUAL OF SOCIAL AND BUSINESS FORMS, by Thomas E. Hill, 1882: pages 8, 9.

*   *   *

Albert Einstein quotation from pamphlet of International Physicians for the Prevention of Nuclear War.

Robert Burton quotation from FAMILIAR QUOTATIONS by John Bartlett, 9th edition, Little, Brown & Co., 1891.

*   *   *

Graphics assistance and reproduction by DYNAMIC PRINTERS, of West Chester, Pennsylvania 19380.

*   *   *